THE ROYAL CODE

CONNOR WHITELEY

No part of this book may be reproduced in any form or by any electronic or mechanical means. Including information storage, and retrieval systems, without written permission from the author except for the use of brief quotations in a book review.

This book is NOT legal, professional, medical, financial or any type of official advice.

Any questions about the book, rights licensing, or to contact the author, please email connorwhiteley@connorwhiteley.net

Copyright © 2022 CONNOR WHITELEY

All rights reserved.

DEDICATION
Thank you to all my readers without you I couldn't do what I love.

THE ROYAL CODE

Returning to where everything began, Cato smiled a little as he remembered this was the centre of humanity. From here all the decisions were made. So, there was no better place to return to now.

As Cato walked along the immensely long white polished marble floor towards the even bigger throne, made of pure crystal and diamonds, in the middle of a raised platforms tens of metres away. Cato heard his light footsteps in his leather boots echoed loudly in this empty throne room.

As he passed the cold dull white marble pillars that rose high into the heavens and ornate paintings on the ceiling. Cato had to smile as he remembered him and his sister playing on the smooth cold floor with their toys as children. Then the maids moaning to themselves at the mess they made on the freshly mopped floor. Those were the days.

Cato turned his head slightly to see in-between the marble pillars and he rolled his eyes as he saw his father still had those horrible murals of ancient warriors. It wasn't like Cato didn't appreciate these warriors. After all they had saved the Realm a few times. Cato just hated the colours and the condition they were in. The least his father could do was giving these murals a lick of paint or gold.

Forcing his attention away, Cato kept walking with his loud footsteps towards the small raised marble platform ahead. Granted Cato never understood his father's obsession with white marble, it was still good to see the throne room looking great. Unlike these horrible murals.

The closer he got to the large crystal throne that looked as if it had grown out of the marble, Cato smelt the odd odour of bitter coffee that left a bitter taste in his mouth. Cato didn't think his father liked coffee, but dismissed the thought and walked up to the crystal throne. And of course his father, the King, wasn't here. Well, he was King of the Realm after all so perhaps he was busy. Cato hoped he wouldn't take long. All he wanted was to get his father to allow him back into the Royal family publicly.

Standing in front of the immense throne, Cato started to feel the majesty of it sink in as he felt chills run up his arms. It was impressive to think how many millions of people would happily give up their freedom just for a brief look at this holy throne and the God-king.

Cato really had no idea why people thought his father was a god. Of course, Cato loved him but his father was very mortal. Which made his stomach churn a little at the thought of seeing him again.

The last time Cato saw the King must have been at least five or six years ago. It would have been the time the King shipped him off to the Dragon Training Facility in the far south.

A part of him knew his father was just protecting him because of the extremely zealous members of the Realm who would have killed Cato for being gay. But the other part of him was still furious that his own father didn't stand up for him and defend him from them. All his father did was give him a new role and shipped him away to one of the farthest points of the Realm.

Definitely not a God-King!

Yet Cato supposed it was a good sign that his father had agreed to meet with him at such short notice.

Although, what puzzled Cato was why his father had insisted and been rather forceful about making sure no one saw him. Granted, Cato was more than happy because it meant he had to sneak in using his stunning dragon Pendra. Sneaking past an army of guards was always fun. Yet the demand was still questionable. Would his father be scared of something?

Shaking the thought away, Cato looked around to see that his father still wasn't here. This was getting ridiculous. Considering how much his father had banged on about its *proper* to be on time. This was hypocrisy clear and simple.

Yet Cato was a dirty piece of scum according to the zealous members of the Realm. So what did Cato know about being proper?

Forcing the thoughts, Cato started to wish he had bought the stunning Pendra in with him. Of course, she wouldn't have fit in the throne room but it was a nice thought. At least it would have given Cato someone to talk to and he could rub her cold blue shiny scales.

However, what Cato really wanted, was to see the beautiful Caden. Even now knowing he, Pendra and Caden's dragon were a few kilometres away. Cato still wanted to look at his beautiful body and that stunningly perfect longish blond hair parted to the left and those amazing crystal blue eyes.

It was still a puzzle why his father had made sure Caden ended up where Cato was based. But Caden's words about him killing and stopping a witch cult to save the Realm. Only then to get arrested and almost executed still made Cato nervous. Caden should have been a Hero to the Realm. Yet the King's stupid attitude that all knowledge about the witch cults must remain secret made that impossible. Maybe Cato would bring that up.

A part of him smiled at the idea that would make it possible for him and Caden to be together after so many close encounters.

At last the loud scream of a door opening made Cato turn around and his face involuntary lit up as his eyes fell upon his father. The old man's impressive long white, red and gold robes of office draped elegantly along the cold white marble. The sound of the King's massive plain golden staff made a loud noise as it tapped against the floor. Then Cato looked at his father's well-aged yet pleasant features.

Cato looked behind his King as the door shut to see no one was there. They were alone.

"Father," Cato greeted.

In a smooth posh voice, the King replied: "It is good to see you my son. But is that all you have to say to me?"

"There is a lot I want to say, Father. You haven't seen me in years. Why the secrecy? Why not be happy that I've returned? You forced me out. You forced me into exile,"

"Cato,"

He looked his Father in the eyes when he spoke his informal name. There was something about the way he said it. Something in those words. Love? Concern? No. Fear and desperation.

The King stretched out his hand.

Cato walked towards his Father.

His Father gently held Cato's face in his smooth perfumed hand.

"My son. My beautiful Cato, I did what I could to protect you. I… thought I did what was right,"

"What Father? Who did you protect me from?"

"What do you know about The Royal Code?"

Cato brushed away his Father's hand and took a few steps back. He rubbed his forehead gently.

"Something about a civil war 600 years ago. The new royal family was only allowed to be crowned if they followed the Royal Code. Wasn't it a type of law that only applied to the royals?"

"Yes, the King about 600 years ago was a tyrant. A truly evil person. The people rose up. They won. They killed his family. There wasn't a Royal family by blood. The people decided to make the most senior Baroness the new Queen. But a fanatical zealot attacked the coronation. Saying the new Queen had to agree to the Royal Code or die. She accepted,"

"Why is this Royal Code such a problem, Father?"

"Because it means I can't do modern innovative things to my people. Like, I can't give them free education or free health care. But more importantly it says you cannot live!"

Cato slowly nodded as he heard the words. He had always known this was true but he just needed to hear it.

"Cato, I sent you away to stop the Royal Code from being acted out,"

"Who enforces the Code?"

"You don't want to know. They will kill you,"

"Father, I am the Lord Dragon Rider. I have killed thousands of orks and foes in my time,"

The King shook his head.

"Cato, the Warden of Faith and his apprentice. They are the two most fanatical people in the Realm. They enforce the Royal Code. If they wanted they could take our army from us and make them wipe us out,"

Cato took a few steps back. His stomach churning and sweat dripped down his forehead at the news.

"Um, can't you just revoke the Code?"

The deep sound of his father laughing almost made Cato jump. He hadn't heard such a unique laugh for years.

"Ha, no. If I do that then I'm rebelling against the will of the Gods. The Warden will kill us,"

Cato looked into his Father's old eyes.

"If I kill them, will I be able to come back?"

"Please don't go after them. I can't lose you,"

"The question,"

"Cato, if they die. I will revoke the Royal Code and I will happily accept you back. But I can't have you back if you're dead,"

Cato started to walk away.

"I'll be fine. I have a dragon,"

"What about Caden and you don't know where to look?"

He stopped. As he remembered how his father had saved and sent Caden to him. His Father was the reason why he got to look at a beautiful boy each day.

"Caden. Thank you. He is beautiful. The witch cults need to be dealt with,"

"The cults are being dealt with. And I'm glad you like him. I thought you would,"

Cato gave his father a boyish teenage smile.

"I don't know where the Warden is, Cato. But he isn't in the Capital. You can make him come here by burning a small extremist church on the outskirts,"

Cato gave his father a quick hug and stormed off.

As he was about to leave the throne room, his Father said: "Cato, if you see any worshippers. Kill them,"

***

The disgusting, foul chants and screams of the worshippers were an assault on Cato's ears.

Standing outside, Cato could feel his anger and rage build within him at these people. These zealots were the reason why he was banished. He didn't want others to know he was gay. It was a part of him. He was never going to throw it in people's faces.

Yet that didn't matter to these people. To these people, he was an unholy abomination who needed to die. But Cato was going to make sure they were the ones who died today.

Looking with disgust at the church, Cato frowned as he studied the rotten wooden panels around the doorway. And the hard grey rocks that were forced to form walls with blood red concrete holding it together.

This entire place was a disgrace to humanity.

Everyone knew the concrete was made from real blood. Blood of the unholy and those who these people deemed as insults to the Gods.

In all honesty, those ideas made Cato laugh. Whilst the Gods were real, Cato had worked alongside them about a decade ago and he knew they despised these people who murdered innocents in their name.

A cold nightly gust made Cato shiver and the sound of rocks falling over made him turn around. To see his stunning dragon Pendra with her smooth blue scales attempting to hide behind some immense gravestones.

One of which laid destroyed at her massive scaly feet.

The faint smell of smoke that left a strange ash taste in his mouth made Cato roll his eyes once more and turn slightly to the right to see Caden's equally stunning dragon Kadien attempting to put out a small fire he had started.

A part of Cato wanted to give the dragon a hug. Poor Kadien had been sick for the past day or two with something akin to a cough. Every time he coughed; he would shoot out some fire.

Amusing, but annoying.

It actually reminded Cato of a time with his sister when they went as children to their first dragon lesson. His sister's dragon coughed and almost burnt her alive!

Cato's poor sister was terrified of dragons for about a year after that. He really needed to go and see his sister once again.

Then the smell of earthy, manly aftershave made

Cato look up at the small fire being put out. And he saw the beautiful Caden.

Cato allowed a massive smile to form on his face as he saw Caden's stunning longish blond hair that was parted perfectly to the right. Then his strong elegant movements were beautiful to look at as he put out the fire. Then Caden looked at Cato. Cato felt his heart skip a beat as he looked into those beautiful crystal blue eyes.

After so many moments and after thinking so much about being with Caden, Cato just wanted to kiss him. He remembered the time in the bandit cave when they had almost kissed. But they were interrupted.

Cato didn't want to be interrupted anymore. He wanted, needed to be with Caden and that is what this was truly about.

"Why don't I just torch ya target, Catty?" Pendra spoke in her usual common tongue but really didn't match her impressive and majestic appearance.

"I do agree with my fellow dragon. It is far more effective for us dragons to burn this foul place down," Kadien said.

Cato loved how these two contrasted each other.

"I agree with the dragons," Caden added.

Just hearing his velvety manly voice made a chill run-down Cato's back.

"As much as I love you all, we need to burn this place down. But there's a relic I want first,"

Caden rolled his eyes.

"Caden, do you know the history of this foul church?" Cato asked.

"Cato you know I'm not cultured,"

Cato playfully hit Pendra as she started laughing.

"We know that. But this place was built on an ancient Witch Cult site. The rumours say this Cult had an artefact that could shatter the earth on the field of battle,"

"Really, Catty? That sound a bit of a long shot. I don't know about ya but I wanna burn this place,"

"The relic is a hammer inside the church behind the altar,"

Caden walked over to Cato and placed a manipulative arm around his waist.

Cato had to smile as he could feel his body warm seep into his clothes.

"And how do you plan to get the Hammer? Two gays walking into a church- what could go wrong?"

Cato sadly pushed Caden away.

"Come now, former Commander, we're both two of the best fighters in the Realm. I know I can kill some zealots. Can you?"

Caden smiled and nodded.

"Pendra, Kadien. Torch the place on our signal. If anyone comes out, kill them,"

Both dragons nodded.

Putting up their hoods and making sure their weapons were covered, Cato led them inside.

His heart was racing and his stomach churned as he walked into this foul place. He would happily kill each and every one of these zealots to protect Caden and his Father. But Cato needed to have control.

As he entered the church, Cato stopped for a brief second to stare at these pointless crowds that stood on either side of an aisle. Leading straight to the altar.

This place was foul and disgusting. The smell of these zealots was horrific. It was a mixture of sweat, faeces and urine. Cato wanted to gag with each breath.

Starting to walk towards the altar, that was nothing more than a solid gold table with an immense silver hammer the size of a man on top, Cato noticed the zealots were all wearing long black cloaks. He managed to see some of their flesh. They all showed long deep cuts from their various religious rituals.

Some of these disgusting people looked as if they were about to die from starvation or blood loss.

Whilst Cato had never had a problem with people self-harming, and he had always tried to help his friends who did it. And show his friends that they didn't need to cut themselves. Doing it for a pointless religious rite was an offence on his friends that had suffered so much.

Continuing to walk towards the altar, Cato started to breathe shallower as the smell was becoming too much as he felt the rough, rocky floor beneath him.

In front of him at the end of the isle of the zealots stepped out a man in a long blood red robe with two long scythes. Dripping fresh dark red blood from a recent sacrifice to Gods and Goddesses that didn't want their worship.

Cato needed to think.

Was this man a threat?

Someone grabbed Cato's wrist.

He stopped. Taking a deep breath.

Cato turned his head to see a woman staring at him in horror.

The woman screamed all types of disgraceful homophobic words.

Cato whipped out his double bladed staff and

slashed her throat.

Caden whipped out his two longswords.

All the zealots screamed as one their unholy, cruel words at what Caden and Cato were.

The Zealots grabbed their swords and rifles.

They charged at Cato.

Cato panicked at the thought of losing Caden.

Now was not the time for romantic thoughts.

A group charged at him.

Cato slashed and lashed his staff at them.

They screamed as their bodies were ripped in two.

Their blood sprayed across the floor.

Cato smashed his staff into the chests of more foes.

Their bones crushed as the staff whacked into them.

More foes came.

The Lord Dragon Rider kicked, punched, and slashed at the foes.

Their bodies fell with a thud.

Cato smashed his boots onto their heads.

Brain matter and blood squirted everywhere.

More Zealots screamed and cursed Cato as he slaughtered them.

Corpses littered the church floor.

A sword slashed against Cato's back.

His leather armour was sliced away.

Revealing his bare body.

This only made the foes were angry and rageful.

Cato had to rapidly dodge tens of powerful attacks.

He heard them scream their tainted words at him.

How dare he show his sinful skin in this place!
The temperature shot up.
Sweat poured from Cato's body.
He quickly looked up.
The wooden roof was ablaze.
He cursed under his breath.
The dragons weren't meant to attack yet.
The foes renew their attack.
A rifle fired.
Cato felt a bullet graze his arm.
He bit down the pain.
The Lord Dragon Rider whipped his staff around in a wide arc.
Lashing tens of throats.
Blood flooded onto the ground.
Cato spun around.
He looked at the altar.
The man in the red robe stared at him.
Cato charged.
The man threw a scythe at Cato.
He dodged it.
Caden screamed.
Cato turned.
He saw a mob of zealots hacking away at something.
Cato went to charge over.
Several flaming beams collapsed in front of him.
Cato wanted to jump over.
He couldn't.
Loud footsteps came from behind.
He spun around. Rising up his staff.
He blocked an attack.
The man in red smiled.
Cato needed to hurry. He had to save Caden.

He whacked the man with the end of his staff.

The man fell to the floor.

Cato rushed over.

The man did something too quick to see.

He thrusted his staff hard into the man's chest.

Before ripping it out.

For good measure, Cato smashed his boot into the man's head.

It cracked like an egg.

Cato felt something running down his abs.

He looked down to see a scythe inside his stomach. Multiple streams of blood dripped from the wound.

His entire body erupted in a symphony of pain as he realised what had happened.

Maybe he was too focused on making sure Caden was okay. Or hoping to get back to him in time but Cato sank to his knees.

Smoke filled the air as the church was consumed by the fire.

Forcing himself back up, Cato looked over at the altar. The Hammer was still there.

Despite the immense pain from the scythe, Cato forced himself to walk over to the altar.

He screamed as he walked.

With each step he could feel the scythe twisting and cutting away at his organs.

He got to the altar and he forced himself to grab the Hammer. It felt cold and damp in his hand.

Looking at the hammer, Cato noted a strange symbol on the head of the Hammer. It was some sort of plant wrapping around a person.

An immense roar filled the church as the roof collapsed above the altar.

Cato shot back with the hammer.

He landed hard on his back.

The hard rough rocky ground burned his back as he laid there.

He screamed in agony as the scythe was knocked out of his wound slightly.

The blood started to flow quicker.

All Cato wanted in that moment was to know if Caden was okay. He couldn't die without knowing if the person he loved was okay. He needed Caden.

With his vision starting to become blurred, Cato looked at the Hammer. Something was different. Something was strange.

Forcing himself to focus on it, Cato saw it was broken. A large crack almost split it in two.

For some unknown reason, Cato grabbed it and smashed the hammer onto the ground with all of his remaining strength. Blood pumped out of the wound.

The Hammer shattered.

There was something in the shards though.

Cato went to reach it.

His vision went black.

His body went limp.

He could barely hear and feel as he heard distant voices.

They were panicked.

Something smooth, cold, and scaly touched him.

Cato's wound burned and he tried to scream but his mind finally went black.

***

With his eyes slowly opening, Cato felt his body weak and covered in some sort of fine silky cloth. He smelt strong toxic chemicals.

When his eyes opened fully, he blinked rapidly as

direct sunlight filled his room and eyes. He heard someone walk across hard stone flooring to cover the window.

When the sun was gone, Cato saw he was tightly dressed in blood-soaked linens lying on a white silk covered bed.

Cato rolled his eyes in both relief and frustration at being stuck in this hospital chamber. He tried to move but he was too tightly wrapped in the linens. And each movement was agony.

The horrible stench of chemicals filled the entire chamber, and they left the worse taste possible in Cato's mouth.

Then he remembered someone else was with him.

A part of him wanted it to be his Father or Sister. He needed his family. He needed to report on the church. Well, he needed to find out about the church first of all. Was he successful or not?

Then the most important thought came into his mind.

"Caden!" he shouted, forcing himself up.

Cato felt wounds pop and reopen at his dramatic move. Pain flooded his skin, but a pair of warm gentle hands grabbed his and held them.

A friendly and beautiful face appeared and helped Cato to get comfortable in his hospital bed once again.

A part of him thought he should say something, but he didn't. Cato just wanted to look at Caden's beautiful hair and face and he wanted to stare into those stunning crystal blue eyes.

"How?" Cato managed after a minute or two of admiring Caden.

"Kadien and Pendra,"

Cato nodded as he took a deep breath to help with the pain.

Caden continued as he helped Cato's head onto the soft feather filled pillow.

"It turns out Kadien sneezed and coughed at the same time. Catching the church alight. Pendra tried to stop the flames but… it spread too quick,"

"You screamed. I thought I…"

Caden stroked Cato's hand gently.

"I'm a former Commander of the Realm. It takes more than a stab wound to kill me. Anyway then the dragons stormed in and saved me. Then we saved you,"

"How?" Cato asked trying to sit up but Caden forced him back down.

"What was that weird symbol on the Hammer's head? It's all you were muttering about when you were unconscious,"

Cato smiled for some reason.

"That Witch Cult that was there. It wasn't a warrior Cult. These Witches weren't fighters. They were healers. Amazing healers. They made some extremely powerful medicines,"

"What? So, they made a fake hammer to hide some?"

Cato nodded.

Caden leaned over Cato and stared at him.

"You said something else in your muttering state,"

"What?"

"You said you loved me,"

Cato stayed silent. He wanted to kick himself for saying it. This was no life for Caden. Cato was hated and a target for the Warden of Faith and whoever his apprentice was. They would certainly kill him. How could he bring Caden into his fight?

"Caden, I do love you. I want to be with you. But until the Royal Code is revoked and the Warden is dead. We can't be. And I... I don't want anything to happen to you in this fight,"

Caden laughed for a moment.

"We've fought Orks, Bandits and now Zealots together. We can handle some Warden if we do it together. And our dragons will help of course. What do you say, Cato?

Despite the pain and the tightness of the linens, Cato grabbed Caden's tunic pulled it close.

Their mouths locked.

GET YOUR FREE AND EXCLUSIVE SHORT STORY NOW! LEARN ABOUT NEMESIO'S PAST!

https://www.subscribepage.com/fireheart

About the author:

Connor Whiteley is the author of over 60 books in the sci-fi fantasy, nonfiction psychology and books for writer's genre and he is a Human Branding Speaker and Consultant.

He is a passionate warhammer 40,000 reader, psychology student and author.

Who narrates his own audiobooks and he hosts The Psychology World Podcast.

All whilst studying Psychology at the University of Kent, England.

Also, he was a former Explorer Scout where he gave a speech to the Maltese President in August 2018 and he attended Prince Charles' 70th Birthday Party at Buckingham Palace in May 2018.

Plus, he is a self-confessed coffee lover!

OTHER SHORT STORIES BY CONNOR WHITELEY

Blade of The Emperor
Arbiter's Truth
The Bloodied Rose
Asmodia's Wrath
Heart of A Killer
Emissary of Blood
Computation of Battle
Old One's Wrath
Puppets and Masters
Ship of Plague
Interrogation
Edge of Failure
One Way Choice
Acceptable Losses
Balance of Power
Good Idea At The Time
Escape Plan
Escape In The Hesitation
Inspiration In Need
Singing Warriors
Dragon Coins
Dragon Tea
Dragon Rider
Knowledge is Power
Killer of Polluters
Climate of Death
Sacrifice of the Soul
Heart of The Flesheater

Heart of The Regent
Heart of The Standing
Feline of The Lost
Heart of The Story
The Family Mailing Affair
Defining Criminality
The Martian Affair
A Cheating Affair
The Little Café Affair
Mountain of Death
Prisoner's Fight
Claws of Death
Bitter Air
Honey Hunt
Blade On A Train
City of Fire
Awaiting Death
Poison In The Candy Cane
Christmas Innocence
You Better Watch Out
Christmas Theft
Trouble In Christmas
Smell of The Lake
Problem In A Car
Theft, Past and Team

Other books by Connor Whiteley:

The Fireheart Fantasy Series
Heart of Fire
Heart of Lies
Heart of Prophecy
Heart of Bones
Heart of Fate

City of Assassins (Urban Fantasy)
City of Death
City of Marytrs
City of Pleasure
City of Power

Agents of The Emperor
Return of The Ancient Ones
Vigilance
Angels of Fire

The Garro Series- Fantasy/Sci-fi
GARRO: GALAXY'S END
GARRO: RISE OF THE ORDER
GARRO: END TIMES
GARRO: SHORT STORIES
GARRO: COLLECTION
GARRO: HERESY
GARRO: FAITHLESS
GARRO: DESTROYER OF WORLDS
GARRO: COLLECTIONS BOOK 4-6

GARRO: MISTRESS OF BLOOD
GARRO: BEACON OF HOPE
GARRO: END OF DAYS

Winter Series- Fantasy Trilogy Books
WINTER'S COMING
WINTER'S HUNT
WINTER'S REVENGE
WINTER'S DISSENSION

Miscellaneous:
RETURN
FREEDOM
SALVATION

www.ingramcontent.com/pod-product-compliance
Lightning Source LLC
LaVergne TN
LVHW011901060526
838200LV00054B/4468